I'll Be Back Before Midnight!

Peter Colley

A SAMUEL FRENCH ACTING EDITION

SAMUELFRENCH.COM
SAMUELFRENCH-LONDON.CO.UK

I'll Be Back Before Midnight! was commissioned by James Roy for the Blyth Summer Festival. First performance was July 3rd, 1979.

Cast of Characters
(in order of appearance)

Greg Sanderson .... *Peter Snell*
Jan Sanderson .... *Angie Gei*
George Willowby....................... *Peter Elliot*
Laura Sanderson....................... *Kate Trotter*

Director............................... *Keith Batten*
Designer............................... *Tony Abrams*
Lighting .... *John Hughes*
Sound............................ *Bjarne Christensen*
Stage Manager...................... *Marcia Muldoon*

THE PLACE

A farmhouse in the country

THE TIME

ACT ONE

Scene One
An evening in early spring

Scene Two
The next morning

Scene Three
That night

ACT TWO

Scene One
A few moments later

Scene Two
Evening, a week later

Scene Three
That night, just before midnight

THE SETTING

The living room of a large farmhouse. The house is over a hundred years old and appears to have been built in more prosperous times. The scale of the doors and windows suggests a grandeur that has long disappeared. The wallpaper is peeling and grimy and the furniture worn and dusty. The main feature of the room is a large doorway, upstage centre, which leads to a stairway and the front door. The bottom of the stairs can be seen framed in the doorway, and also a small window is visible on the back wall. The doorway can be closed off by two large sliding doors, heavily built of hardwood, and can be locked from inside the living room. A swinging door leads to the kitchen and there is also a large hatch which permits access from the living room to the kitchen. This hatch slides vertically. A large bay window dominates one side of the room and the entire bay can be closed off by heavy drapes. On the other side of the room is an old top-loading pot-bellied stove. The furniture consists of a sofa, coffee table, armchair, and a round dinette table with two chairs. A desk sits in one corner. There is a bookcase on either side of the double doorway, one containing a large number of academic-looking books, the other a stereo system. Beside the armchair is a small table with a telephone on it, and the sofa has an end-table with a strange contraption on it. This contraption has a long spring-loaded arm with a rock clamped to the end of it. On the wall are several Stone Age implements and weapons, and a display case of flint arrowheads. On another wall, quite high up, is a double-barrelled shotgun mounted on a gun rack. There are a number of small table lamps and sconces on the wall, but the main lighting comes from an overhead chandelier whose intensity can be controlled by a wall-mounted dimmer switch. The floor is varnished wood with an old, patterned carpet between the sofa and arm chair.

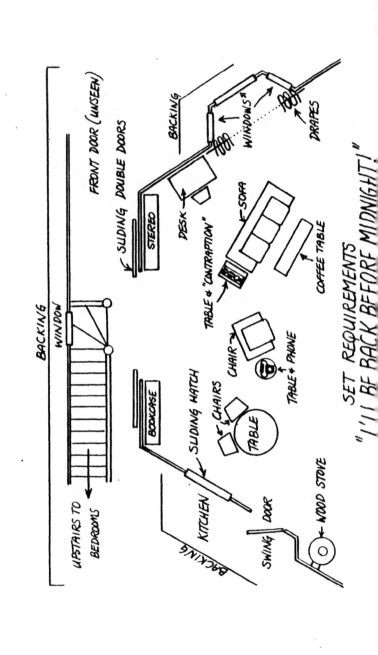

SET REQUIREMENTS
"I'll BE BACK BEFORE MIDNIGHT!"

PLAYWRIGHT'S NOTES

When I first decided to try my hand at a comedy-thriller it was my intention to have some fun with the genre. An old farmhouse in the depths of some rural wilderness seemed like a good place to start. Filling the house with ghosts, or at least rumours of them, was the obvious next step and then parachute in a typically neurotic city couple to give the ghosts someone to work on. The wife, fresh from a nervous breakdown, has "victim" written all over her, and the husband — an insensitive jogging archeologist — obviously isn't going to be much help in a crisis. Add to this a bluff, hearty local farmer and a beautiful but wicked "other woman", and I reckoned I'd covered most of the bases for an entertaining spoof.

What ultimately happened rather surprised me. While the comedy in the play always lurked nearby in the shadows, the characters themselves were forever trying to escape from the clichéd constraints into which they had been placed. To a certain extent I let them go, and tried to make them as truthful as possible within the inherent craziness of the genre. After watching the play I am often gratified to see how much the audience relates to the characters as real people, on numerous occasions shouting spontaneous warnings to the performers during the more frightening scenes. Of course this play is not heavy psycho-drama either. The key to the playing (and the reading) of the piece is to keep the sense of the fun in balance with a terrifying reality. The audience should walk a tightrope of hysteria — not knowing whether the next minute will contain a laugh or a scream.

Another comment I have heard from people who have

read the play and then later have seen it performed is: "I had no idea it would be so frightening". Perhaps my description of the action is a little dry, but in a playscript of this type one relies heavily on the director and the lighting and sound technicians to set the mood and to orchestrate the timing of events. I have tried to be as descriptive as I can without resorting to monumental prose, but the stage directions are written primarily to assist the director and the actors rather than the reading public. However, if you should find yourself alone in a farmhouse on a windswept moor, and it's four in the morning and you can't sleep because of the thunderstorm that's rattling around your ears .... that would be the perfect time to pull up a candle and read "I'LL BE BACK BEFORE MIDNIGHT!".

Peter Colley

I'LL BE BACK BEFORE MIDNIGHT

ACT I
SCENE 1

SETTING: The living room of an large old farmhouse. (For a detailed description of the set see the previous pages.)

AT RISE: The stage is totally dark, except for a shaft of moonlight slanting across the room from the windows. The sound of a car can be heard in the distance and the light from the car headlights briefly illuminates the room. The sound of the wheels coming up a gravel driveway getting louder and then coming to a halt. The engine stops, the car doors slam, and after a moment there is the sound of a key in a lock and a door opening. Voices can be heard in the darkness as two people enter the darkened room.

WOMAN'S VOICE. The light won't work.

MAN'S VOICE. The electricity's off, Jan. Don't move, I know exactly where it is. *(The MAN moves and then trips and sprawls headlong in the dark, tipping over furniture as he falls)* Damn!

WOMAN'S VOICE. Are you all right?

MAN'S VOICE. Yes. Darn thing! The fuse box is under

9

the stairs somewhere. *(There are more sounds of fumbling around in the dark)* **Here it is.** *(The lights go on to reveal JAN SANDERSON in the living room. JAN is a woman in her late twenties, she is pretty but not exceptionally so. She carries two paper grocery bags. She looks around the room. GREG SANDER-SON enters from the hallway. He is in his early thirties, and his manner and dress are those of a rather stuffy intellectual, although under that exterior is a quite handsome man with a good physique)*

GREG. Well? What do you think?

JAN. *(She hates it)* Oh, Greg, it's ... quaint.

GREG. I knew you'd love it. It's just the place for us, Jan.

JAN. Where's the kitchen?

GREG. Through here. *(GREG goes into the kitchen through a swing door and pulls up a sliding hatch)* Look, you can pass stuff right through. *(JAN looks through the hatch)* I know — the fridge and stove are prehistoric, but they work. *(GREG comes back into the living room. JAN shivers a little)*

JAN. Have you turned the heat on yet? It's quite chilly in here.

GREG. Well, you don't exactly turn the heat on. You sort of chop it up, shove it in and throw in a match.

JAN. A wood stove?

GREG. Real country living. Evenings curled up by a crackling fire...

JAN. But you've never used a wood stove before.

GREG. Sure, I have. It's just like a barbeque. *(Lifts the lid off the stove)* I already put the wood in. *(Gets a small plastic container)*

JAN. What's that?

GREG. Gasoline. It's cheaper than barbeque fluid.

JAN. I thought people used paper and twigs and things like that?

GREG. That was before science discovered more combustible materials. *(Pours the gasoline on top of the wood)* You leave it for a moment to soak in...

JAN. You know, a wood stove might be fun.

GREG. Then drop in a match, and very soon you have heat. *(He lights a match and drops it in, replacing the cover over the hole. There is a loud explosion in the stove and the hole cover flies into the air. JAN screams)*

GREG. *(Prodding the stove)* Hmm. This system still has a few flaws in it.

JAN. I thought this was supposed to calm my nerves!

GREG. *(Still examining the stove and muttering to himself)* Of course, it's an enclosed space. Stupid of me... *(JAN looks around nervously)*

JAN. I think I'll make us some coffee. Is there any coffee in the house?

GREG. Lots. But you sit down, I'll make it.

JAN. *(She stops him)* Do you know how long it's been since I indulged in the simple pleasure of making my husband a coffee? So you take a seat and relax. Do we have any cream?

GREG. Yes. There's some in that bag. *(JAN takes the grocery bags into the kitchen. She pokes her head through the hatch)*

JAN. From now on I'll make you all the coffee you like. *(JAN's face disappears and GREG moves around the living room, observing with some satisfaction the collection of prehistoric arrowheads and axes that adorn the walls. He picks up a rock and a magnifying glass from his desk and sits and examines it. JAN appears at the kitchen door)*

JAN. Greg ... are you glad I'm back?

GREG. Of course I am.

JAN. I want this to be a new start for us. I know it was my fault, mostly, but I really feel better.

GREG. It wasn't all you. The doctors said if I'd only communicated a little more...

JAN. If I do anything that annoys you, you must tell me. Don't keep it inside.

GREG. I won't. I've changed, you know. And out here it will all be different. We'll have time for each other.

JAN. I wish you'd told me though.

GREG. Told you what?

JAN. That you'd rented a place in the country.

GREG. But it makes so much sense. I can take my sabbatical and you can... recover. Besides, I wanted it to be a surprise.

JAN. But there are no people around here.

GREG. Sure there are. This isn't the wilderness you know. There's farms all around and the village is only five miles away. Look, it's your first day out of the hospital so naturally you're feeling tense. Tell you what, I'll put some music on. That'll relax you. *(Gets up and goes to the stereo)* What would you like?

JAN. I don't mind. Something soothing. *(GREG puts a record on, but rather than being soothing the music could be interpreted by a nervous person as having a chillingly ominous quality to it. JAN tries to ignore it)*

JAN. You know, as we drove out here this evening, every town we passed I kept thinking: "this is it, this must be it!" But the towns got smaller, then became villages and still we hadn't arrived. *(GREG moves behind Jan. He takes the suitcase and goes upstairs. JAN does not see him go and just keeps talking)* Then the sun went down and everything went so black ... all that was left was the car headlights along the road. It was like going down a long dark tunnel. I mean... I never thought I'd miss the old neon lights and the noise, but I do. Amazing. *(The music hits a particularly spooky chord. JAN looks toward the stereo uncomfortably. She realizes for the first time she is alone)* Greg? *(She gets up and looks around nervously)* Greg, what are you doing? *(She dashes over to the stereo and turns it off)* Greg! Where are you? *(She is beginning to panic. The silence is terrifying her)* Greg! Greg! *(In her fear JAN has backed up against the kitchen hatch. Suddenly it opens right behind her with a loud jolt. She screams. GREG pops his head through the hatch and smiles)*

GREG. What's the matter?

JAN. You nearly scared me to death!

GREG. I was just putting your luggage away. There's a back stairway.

JAN. Oh! I thought you'd ... it's crazy I... *(Embarrassed)* Look, it's the first time I've been left alone, that's all. I'll be all right. *(JAN takes some pills out of her handbag)*

GREG. It's a natural reaction, Jan. Once we've settled in...

JAN. It's the isolation of this place! I just need people around me right now.

GREG. Ah! Well, there's George just across the way. He's the farmer I rented this place from. He's a real character, you'll love him, and when Sis arrives you'll have her around to talk to.

JAN. What!

GREG. I said — ah — when Sis arrives you'll have someone to...

JAN. Oh, Greg, no! Not Laura!

GREG. She's just dropping in for a little while.

JAN. But Greg, I need to spend some time with you. Surely she understands that.

GREG. She won't be staying long.

JAN. That's what she said the last time, and you know what happened then.

GREG. She likes you. She wants to patch things up between you.

JAN. She likes *you,* not me.

GREG. I can't understand your attitude towards her. Look, she's moving out west, this may be the last chance I get to see her for ... years maybe.

JAN. She's going out west?

GREG. Yes. She's even given up her job, sold her car, and everything. How could I tell her not to come?

JAN. I'm not ready for it, Greg ... really I'm not.

GREG. I have to go out and collect flints every day, and then there's my running. You'll be glad she's around.

JAN. Frankly she's the last person I want to see right now.

GREG. Well, I couldn't stop her now even if I wanted to.

JAN. What do you mean?

GREG. The bus has already left, I think.

JAN. She's on the bus now!!

GREG. Unless it's late.

JAN. She's coming here tonight! I don't believe it! How

did you let her talk you into that?

GREG. . Really, Jan ... you misjudge her completely.

JAN. *(Hurt)* She'll take over this whole house. She'll take over you again.

GREG. It's not going to be like that at all. Try it for me, Jan.

JAN. If I can't take it you'll send her away?

GREG. Of course, but it'll be O.K., I promise. *(Trying to cheer her up)* Now go and get that coffee, it should be ready by now.

JAN. *(Reluctantly)* All right. I'm not looking forward to it though. *(JAN goes into the kitchen. GREG picks up one of his rocks and the magnifying glass, and continues to examine it. JAN enters with a mug of coffee and goes over to Greg)*

JAN. Where would you like it? *(Before GREG has a chance to answer there is a loud knock at the door and JAN, startled, drops the mug of coffee right on Greg's lap. GREG jumps up in pain and the mug tumbles to the floor. GEORGE WILLOWBY sticks his head into the room. He is an enormous, ruddy-faced farmer in his fifties. He is dressed in overalls, a cap and muddy boots. GEORGE has a craggy old face, and what little hair he has left is grey. He talks lazily, as if leaning up against a fence on a warm day, but punctuates his speech with a loud, infectious, but slightly demented laugh)*

GEORGE. Hello! Hello! How are the love-birds? *(JAN dashes into the kitchen for a cloth)*

GREG. Ah, George ... come in.

GEORGE. Thought I'd drop over. Saw the lights. *(GREG is doubled up in pain. GEORGE notices this)* Are you all right?

GREG. Don't mind me, George. *(GREG continues to hob-*

ble around in pain. GEORGE watches this, not quite understanding what's going on. JAN enters with a cloth, sees the mug on the floor, picks it up and disappears into the kitchen again)

GEORGE. So, Mr. Sanderson ... this must be your new bride.

GREG. Well, she's not exactly new, George.

GEORGE. I know what you mean, Mr. Sanderson. Very few of them are these days. I'm liberal minded, though, so what the heck. *(JAN enters and tries to rub the coffee stain off the fly of Greg's trousers. GEORGE observes this carefully. GREG tries to stop her)*

GREG. Jan, this is George.

JAN. *(Flustered)* Pleased to meet you. *(Exits to the kitchen with the cloth. GEORGE goes to Greg and nudges him.)*

GEORGE. You'll have your hands full there! *(Roars with laughter, and goes over to warm himself in front of the stove, which he soon discovers is not lit. JAN comes back in from the kitchen and sits by Greg)*

GEORGE. So. When was the wedding?

JAN. What wedding?

GEORGE. But, I thought...

JAN. We've been married for six years.

GEORGE. Six years!

JAN. We just haven't been together for a while.

GEORGE. Ah ... I see... Well, is everything all right here?

GREG. Yes. Fine.

GEORGE. It's still a bit dusty, ain't it? *(He licks his lips)* I can always feel it. Dries the mouth right out. Yes sir. Very dry.

GREG. *(Finally gets the hint)* Oh! Would you like a drink,

George? *(George's eyes light up)*

JAN. The coffee's ready.

GEORGE. Ah ... coffee. My doctor says I shouldn't drink coffee. Too stimulating, you know.

JAN. Hot chocolate?

GEORGE. Brings me out in a rash.

GREG. We do have some whisky.

GEORGE. Now you're talking! Not too much, eh? Just a small mug would be fine. *(GREG gets a bottle of whisky out of a sideboard and goes into the kitchen to get a mug. JAN motions GEORGE to sit down, which he does)*

GEORGE. Yup. It's a good old house. Solid, no leaks or nothing. I bought it a few years back for my boy, Robert, but he's not too keen on farming, so I just rents it out. Yup, I think you'll enjoy it here. The last bunch sure did. They'd still be here now if it weren't for the ghosts.

JAN. The ghosts!

GEORGE. Well, I don't believe in them myself, Mrs. Sanderson, but these were city folks and they'd read too many books.

JAN. What ghosts?

GEORGE. 'Bout fifty years ago there was a ghastly murder took place in this very room. Was a young woman, 'bout your age. *(GREG returns with a mug of whisky and gives it to George)*

GREG. What was that?

JAN. Greg ... there was a murder committed in this very room!

GEORGE. A long time ago, eh!

GREG. How fascinating.

GEORGE. I hope you folks don't believe in ghosts.

GREG. The only thing I believe in is science. To me a ghost is just a chemical in someone's brain. *(GREG saunters over to his desk and starts to potter around with his rocks, keeping one ear on the conversation)*

GEORGE. I'm glad you feel that way. This house has scared off a lot of people over the years. It's the ghosts that scare them mainly... *(GEORGE takes a swig of whisky)* ...and the blood.

JAN. Blood!

GEORGE. There's a red stain that appears on the floor. It was this young woman they say. They found her body right there, lying in a pool of blood. They say that whenever there's a murder 'round these parts that the floor turns red.

JAN. Who murdered her?

GEORGE. Well, the story goes like this: there was a hermit who lived up where the quarry is now. He was deformed... quite grotesque apparently. *(Very seriously, to Jan)* I guess that's why he became a hermit. *(Roars with laughter)* Well... the farmer who lived here sold the mining rights to this company who wanted to start quarrying up there. The old hermit, though, wouldn't move, so they drove him off. But that very night he crept back... forced open that window and stabbed the farmer's daughter to death right in this room ... just before midnight.

JAN. Did they ever catch him?

GEORGE. No, they never did, but a lot of folks 'round here claim they've seen him.

GREG. *(Laughing cynically)* Surely he'd have died long ago.

GEORGE. This is his ghost that people see. They say you should never go up to the quarry at night, and you should never stay in this house. *(Seriously, to Jan)* I shouldn't be telling you that, should I? *(GEORGE bursts into gales of laughter, JAN goes to the window and looks out nervously)*

JAN. They actually see this hermit?

GEORGE. Well, first they hear him. It's kind of like a heartbeat sound, like... well ... a heart, but louder. Then he's supposed to appear with this long bloodstained knife...

JAN. Oh, my God!

GREG. I think you should change the subject, George.

GEORGE. I'm sorry. Makes you nervous, does it?

GREG. It's Jan, she has a very vivid imagination.

JAN. I'm all right. It's fascinating, really.

GEORGE. Don't worry you none?

JAN. No, not at all. *(GEORGE finishes his whisky and inadvertantly puts the mug down on Greg's "contraption". The mechanical arm swings down and demolishes George's mug with a loud crash. JAN and GEORGE jump in shock)*

GEORGE. What in tarnation!

GREG. Carefull, George! That's one of my ... machines.

GEORGE. Nearly chopped my hand off. What's it for?

GREG. It's for chipping and splitting flints.

GEORGE. Flints?

GREG. For making tools. Like this axe. *(GREG gets a flint axe, bound with leather, off the wall and shows it to George)* It's part of my studies. I'm researching how men used to make these Stone Age tools. This machine is part of my experiments on lithic technology.

GEORGE. *(Quite lost)* Ah.

GREG. The study of making things out of rocks.

GEORGE. Oh. So, that's what you and that other fella do up in the quarry.

GREG. Yes. That's Jan's father. He's the head of the department at the university. I designed this machine to help me understand the principles behind the fracturing of microcrystalline silicates. Let me show you how it works...

JAN. *(As gently as possible)* Greg, I'm sure Mr. Willowby isn't interested in getting a run-down on your Ph.D. *(GREG looks at Jan, obviously hurt by that remark. GEORGE notices this and jumps in)*

GEORGE. No, no! I'm very interested in your scholarly pursuits. I'm a bit of a scholar myself, and my boy, Robert, is very bright too. Why, I've heard him talk for hours without understanding a word he's said.

JAN. What do you study, George?

GEORGE. Well, I read a lot. A good mystery is my tonic. Love a good mystery. *(GREG puts the flint axe back on the wall. As he does so, he looks at the clock on his desk)*

GREG. Good God! Look at the time. I've got to get out to the road to flag down the bus.

GEORGE. Someone comin' in on the seven-thirtyfive?

GREG. My sister, Laura.

GEORGE. *(Pulling out a pocket watch)* It'll just be comin' over the hill. Many's the time I've met my boy, Robert, on the seven-thirtyfive.

GREG. *(Looking out of the window)* I think I can see the lights.

GEORGE. You'd better hurry.

JAN. Would you like another drink, George?

GEORGE. Thanks. Good stuff this. *(JAN takes George's*

mug and exits into the kitchen. The moment she has gone GREG goes over to George and whispers to him)

GREG. George, there's a couple of things I should mention before I go... *(GREG whispers intently into George's ear. JAN enters with the whisky and sees them. GREG sees her and breaks away from George)* Just checking the directions. Well, I'd better go — don't want to keep Laura waiting. *(GREG exits. GEORGE looks a little uncomfortable)*

GEORGE. Well, I sure hope you like the country life.

JAN. Oh, I'm sure we will. It just takes a little getting used to. I'm a little disoriented, that's all. I find being in the country at night kind of frightening. *(Pause)* Did Greg tell you that I just got out of the hospital? Is that what he told you?

GEORGE. He mentioned something about it. Look, Mrs. Sanderson, I'm sorry about all these ghost stories. There's really nothing to be frightened of 'round here.

JAN. Please understand, I've lived in the city all my life. *(Nervously looking out of the window)* For all I know, there's bears and wolves roaming around out there. *(She looks ot George for reassurance)* There aren't, are there?

GEORGE. What, bears and wolves? *(He laughs)* No, no. There's nothing like that.

JAN. *(Relieved, she sits)* Thank heavens! What about snakes?

GEORGE. There's no poisonous snakes 'round here, and once they catch that leopard there'll be nothing that can hurt you.

JAN. *(Jumps up)* A what?

GEORGE. It escaped from that "Safari Park" thing they got near Hillsborough. Don't worry, it's only a small one. Mind you, it's been eating a lot of livestock.

JAN. Oh, dear! I'm afraid I'm not very good when it comes to animals!

GEORGE. Well, I left you a shotgun. Just in case. *(He points to the old shotgun on the wall)*

JAN. That thing works?

GEORGE. You bet. It's old, but it'll blast that critter into fur balls. Of course, if you can catch it alive there's a reward.

JAN. *(Paces, nervously)* This is all rather too much for me. First the ghost, and now some wild animal is on the loose!

GEORGE. I wouldn't worry about it. It's really very peaceful out here.

JAN. You call this peaceful!

GEORGE. Oh, sure. That ghost stuff was all a long time ago. Nothin' strange has happened 'round here recently. Nothing at all. *(Pause)* Not since Charlie Reese got murdered.

JAN. Murdered!

GEORGE. *(Casually)* Someone lopped his head off with a chain saw.

JAN. Oh, my God! Who did that?

GEORGE. Nobody I knew. Some argument about a tree. But generally folks are quiet 'round here. Not like the city.

JAN. *(Aghast)* Well I never heard of anyone in the city having their head lopped off with a chain saw!

GEORGE. *(Dryly)* That's 'cos country folks' got more imagination. In the city they stick knives in each other and blow their brains out with guns. Dull. In the country you can have a tractor fall on your head, be chopped to pieces in a combine, drown in a silo of grain or drive your snowmobile right through a fence. Just like cheesewire. *(He indicates a wire cutting his throat)* Dozens of ways to catch it, and no two ways the same. I'd take that to knife in the gut anytime. *(There is the sound of a car's horn in the distance. JAN tenses up visibly)* Good of your sister-in-law to come down. Helping you get the place spick and span, eh?

JAN. To be honest with you, George, I wish she wasn't coming.

GEORGE. Oh?

JAN. I'm afraid my sister-in-law and I don't exactly get along. I don't know, maybe I'm just oversensitive. Everyone seems to think I am.

GEORGE. *(Gently)* Nothin' wrong with being sensitive.

JAN. It always seems to get me into trouble.

GEORGE. That's funny. I'm always told I'm not sensitive enough. You can't win, can you?

JAN. I think you're sensitive, George. I can also tell you're a very honest person.

GEORGE. Well, thank you. I've always thought of myself as honest, but you never know. As Sherlock Holmes always says: "It is a great mistake to theorize before you have the facts." I could be a looney for all you know. *(GEORGE laughs dementedly, and then realizes what he's said)* Beg your pardon, Missus. *(The sound of car wheels coming up the driveway. The light from the headlights flashes across the room, and the car comes to a halt. JAN is becoming increasingly nervous)*

JAN. George, are you a very good judge of character?

GEORGE. Not bad, I'd say.

JAN. Would you do me a favour?

GEORGE. Sure.

JAN. It's Laura ... she has this effect on Greg. He seems to change so much when she's around. See if you can...

(There is the sound of the front door opening, and voices. JAN stops talking and looks around nervously) I'll go check the coffee. *(JAN disappears into the kitchen. LAURA SANDERSON enters followed closely by GREG carrying a couple of suitcases. LAURA is a strikingly attractive woman in her thirties, dressed in a perfectly tailored pant suit, looking every inch the sophisticated business woman)*

LAURA. What a beautiful place! *(Sees George)* You must be George.

GEORGE. Right first time.

LAURA. I'm Laura. Greg's sister.

GEORGE. Pleased to meet you. I hope you like it here.

LAURA. I'm sure I will. It's so exciting, I've never lived in the country before.

GEORGE. You'll find lots of nice walks 'round here. Fresh air, straight off the lake. In no time you'll be happy as a pig in shit. *(GEORGE appears totally unaware of what he has just said. GREG and LAURA look at each other and smile at this. JAN enters tentatively from the kitchen)*

LAURA. Hello Jan. You're looking terrific.

JAN. *(Trying to be pleasant)* It's been a long time.

LAURA. It's so nice to see you again. I really wanted to see you in the hospital, but the doctors advised against it. How are you feeling?

JAN. Much better, thanks.

LAURA. I'm really sorry about barging in so soon, but I hope Greg explained.

JAN. He tells me you're going out west.

LAURA. Yes. It's a big step, but I think it'll help my career. *(An awkward pause)* Well, I should take my bags upstairs. *(GREG jumps in eagerly)*

GREG. No, no! Let me take them.

LAURA. Thank you. *(GREG goes upstairs with the bags)*

LAURA. How old is this house, George?

GEORGE. Don't rightly know. 'Been here as long as I can remember.

LAURA. It's probably haunted too.

GEORGE. So they say.

LAURA. I love haunted houses.

GEORGE. You believe in ghosts, eh?

LAURA. No. It's the atmosphere I like.

JAN. I believe in ghosts.

LAURA. *(Looking pointedly at Jan)* Then you'll like this house best of all. *(GREG comes downstairs)*

JAN. I'll get some coffee. Laura, would you like some? It's made.

LAURA. No, thank you.

JAN. Greg?

GREG. Yes, please. *(JAN exits into the kitchen. GREG sits on the sofa near Laura)*

GREG. Well, what do you think?

LAURA. Gorgeous. It looks a lot better now.

GEORGE. Oh, you've seen it before, eh?

LAURA. *(Caught, but unruffled)* No. Better than I imagined it would look.

GEORGE. Ah. *(JAN enters with the coffee)*

JAN. I won't spill it this time.

GREG. Thanks, Jan. *(JAN sits defensively between GREG and LAURA on the sofa. The atmosphere is tense, but everyone is putting on a pleasant face. GREG takes a sip of his coffee and grimaces)* God, that's awful! *(Half-jokingly to Jan)* What are you trying to do, poison me to death?

JAN. I'm sorry, Greg.

GREG. *(Laughing, to the others)* It must have perked too long. *(JAN suddenly becomes very emotional, and near tears)*

JAN. I'm sorry, Greg. Really, I'm sorry. I don't know how it could have happened!

GREG. It's all right, Jan. It's just a cup of coffee. *(LAURA moves over to Greg and takes his cup)*

LAURA. Let me make it. I know exactly how Greg likes his coffee.

JAN. *(Suddenly flares up)* No! I'll make him his coffee, not you! *(JAN grabs the cup out of Laura's hand and rushes toward the kitchen. GREG intercepts her)*

GREG. It's all right, Jan. It's really not that bad.

LAURA. *(Sweetly)* I was only trying to help.

JAN. *(To Greg)* I'm out of practice, that's all.

GREG. I know. It's perfectly understandable. And Laura was only trying to help.

LAURA. That's all, Jan. Really.

GREG. So why don't you let her make the coffee. *(GREG carefully takes the cup out of Jan's hand and places it in Laura's. JAN is mutely hostile)*

JAN. All right. *(LAURA goes into the kitchen. There is an uncomfortable pause)*

GEORGE. *(Breaking the tension)* That's why I drink whisky! Leave the making to others.

JAN. I'm sorry about that, George. I was being stupid.

GEORGE. *(Comforting)* Hey, I'll bet in a couple of days you'll be making coffee so good even I'd drink it. *(GEORGE smiles at her, trying to cheer her up)* I'm not making any promises, though. *(LAURA returns from the kitchen)*

LAURA. Shouldn't be long now. You know I've really been looking forward to this. No deadlines, no rush.

JAN. *(Almost to herself)* Yes. I was looking forward to it too.

LAURA. That's marvelous. I really want us to be friends, Jan. That's what I've always wanted. *(Holds Greg's hand)* One big happy family.

JAN. Sounds terrific. Shall I play the wife? *(Looking at Laura)* Or shall you? *(LAURA looks a little stung, GREG looks away and shakes his head, and GEORGE, observing all this with disbelief, swigs back his whisky in a gulp as the stage goes to black. Ominous music fades in and continues through the blackout.)*

End of Scene 1

SCENE 2

AT RISE: It is the next morning. The room is empty and the early morning light is filtering through the curtained windows. An alarm clock rings upstairs and is stopped. After a few moments GREG comes downstairs in shorts and a 'T' shirt, carrying his running shoes. He goes into the kitchen and emerges with several bottles of pills and a small can of vegetable juice. He goes to the record player and puts on a record with an up-tempo dance beat. GREG then begins to exercise to the music, gently at first and then really getting into it until he is violently hopping around the room. JAN enters from upstairs wearing a rather dowdy housecoat. She sees Greg exercising and smiles. She goes to the window and throws open the curtains, allowing bright early morning sunshine to fill the room.

JAN. What are you having for breakfast?

GREG. *(Continuing to exercise)* The usual. Vitamins A, D, C, B12, riboflavin, vitamin E. And some minerals: manganese, phosphorous, copper and iron.

JAN. Honey, I'm surprised you don't rust. You should be eating real food. I can see I'm going to have to build you up again ... your diet is ruining you.

GREG. Is there some hidden meaning in that remark? *(GREG stops the record)* Were you referring to last night?

JAN. Oh, that. *(With a smile)* Well, a little raw meat may help that along too.

GREG. It's just been a while, that's all. You don't expect a car to start that's been sitting in the driveway for four months, do you?

JAN. Well, I wasn't much help either, but I still think a good breakfast would work wonders.

GREG. These pills provide me with all the nutrients I need.

JAN. You always loved my cooking. At least try some.

GREG. Tomorrow maybe. It's time for my run. *(JAN sees his running shoes lying on the floor, and grabs them)*

JAN. You're not leaving until I feed you!

GREG. What is this... a compulsive maternal neurosis? *(GREG moves towards her. JAN playfully backs away)* Now, give me those shoes.

JAN. Just think of a barbaric breakfast of bacon and eggs...

GREG. Give them to me! *(JAN coquettishly hides them behind her back)*

JAN. Muffins and fresh coffee... *(GREG appears to be getting into the spirit of the game. He chases her and grabs her. They struggle for the running shoes behind Jan's back. GREG lifts her up in his arms. JAN drops the shoes and kisses him. At that moment LAURA comes down the stairs in a stunning white satin robe, her make-up carefully applied. LAURA gives GREG an icy glare and he hastily puts JAN down. GREG appears embarrassed. He grabs his running shoes and puts them on)*

GREG. 'Morning, Sis. How did you sleep?

LAURA. Terribly. It's too damn quiet. *(JAN smiles at Laura)*

JAN. Since you're up, why don't you have breakfast with me?

LAURA. Thank you. I will. *(JAN exits into the kitchen)*

GREG. *(To Laura)* I was going for a run. It's beautiful at this time of the morning. *(LAURA holds Greg's arm)*

LAURA. Stay and talk with me for a while.

GREG. After I get back maybe. *(GREG moves away from her)*

LAURA. Greg! *(She stops him)* Relax! *(He sits rather reluctantly)* How's your work going?

GREG. Fine.

LAURA. Making progress?

GREG. A bit. *(Pause)*

LAURA. What's the matter?

GREG. I'm sorry. *(Pause)* Look, what happened to that guy you were going with? That account executive. What happened to him?

LAURA. He was only a copywriter. *I'm* an account executive.

GREG. Well, what happened?

LAURA. You know what happened. The same as always happens. Look, what are you bringing that up for?

GREG. I sometimes wonder if you ever really try.

LAURA. *(Moving close to Greg and whispering intensely)* Of course I try! You think it's easy for me after all we've been through. I just can't relate to these men.

GREG. And that's my fault I suppose. *(She does not reply)* And so, as always, you come running back to me.

LAURA. So that's how you see it. Well, you just say the word and I'll go. I'll move to the other side of the continent if that's what you want.

GREG. You'll always come back, Laura.

LAURA. Oh, yes! Well, don't be too sure. I can survive very well on my own. I can make more money in one day than you'll ever make with your stupid rocks! *(GREG glares at her angrily and starts to exit)* Greg..! *(Contrite)* I'm proud of your work, you know that. But you can't expect me to survive out there alone, not after what's happened. *(GREG softens and moves back to Laura when the swing door opens and JAN appears with a tray of coffee and muffins. GREG and LAURA see her and move apart)*

GREG. Well, I'm off. See you later. *(GREG exits and JAN is all smiles. LAURA on the other hand is still smarting from the confrontation with Greg)*

JAN. That is significant. That is really significant.

LAURA. What is?

JAN. Greg hasn't been like that for years. When we first met, oh, we would laugh about everything. He had the craziest sense of humour ... you hardly ever see it these days. He's become so involved in his work. Just then I got a glimpse of the old Greg. I know it must seem like we've had nothing but problems, but we did have some wonderful years. We were very, very happy once. It was when your mother died last fall that our lives were turned inside out. Greg just stopped talking ... he wouldn't say a word for days on end. I tried to help but ended up feeling more and more ... inadequate.

LAURA. *(Thoughtfully)* It was a difficult time for all of us.

JAN. But he handled it so well at first. It was after the funeral that everything changed. *(LAURA flashes Jan a look that hints of the significance of that)*

LAURA. Well ... it takes a while to sink in. Perhaps when he saw the coffin ... it was a very emotional time. You mustn't think of it as a rejection of you. I'm sure he still loved you.

JAN. Really? Did he say so?

LAURA. Well, no. But I'm sure he did.

JAN. All these months of white walls and white people. I'm really hoping that this time...

LAURA. You can't expect things to be exactly as they were, Jan.

JAN. It's the feeling, Laura, that's all I ask. Did you see the way he picked me up in his arms? Why, it's been years since...

LAURA. He did what?

JAN. He picked me up in his arms.

· LAURA. Oh. *(Casually)* Must have been before I came down.

JAN. *(Confused)* No, Laura. You were here ... why ... it was just a few moments ago.

LAURA. What exactly was it he did?

JAN. I'd taken his running shoes ... he chased me ... and picked me up in his arms just like he used to ... but surely you remember?

LAURA. *(Sweetly)* You must be thinking of another time, or perhaps you dreamt it?

JAN. No!

LAURA. I wouldn't worry about it, Jan. It's understandable.

JAN. You think I was hallucinating, don't you?

LAURA. No, I don't, Jan. You've always had a vivid imagination.

JAN. It happened, damn it! You're lying!

LAURA. Well! What can I say? O.K., it happened. It makes no difference to me. *(She gets up)* I think I'll go and get dressed. *(LAURA exits upstairs. JAN appears hurt and per-*

plexed. She walks around for a moment as if trying to re-create what happened between her and Greg. Then she goes to a cupboard and takes out a small portable cassette tape recorder with a microphone attached to it. JAN pops a cassette in it and talks into the microphone)

JAN. Dr. Kate Sinclair. Tape number one, side two, April 15th. Hi Kate. Well, we've only been here a day and I've had a couple of problems. The worst one happened just a moment ago. You see ... I'm convinced I saw Greg do something, but Laura — yes Laura, can you believe that, she's here already — she claims that he didn't. It's so confusing, Kate — do you think I should confront Greg with it? It's just that if he didn't do it ... I know what he'll think. *(The phone rings. JAN goes to the phone and picks it up)* Hello. Who is it? *(As she listens she appears worried)* I said who is it? *(Slams the phone down and retreats from it in horror. LAURA comes downstairs)*

LAURA. Who was it?

JAN. Oh, my God!

LAURA. Well, who was it?

JAN. It was horrible! There was just this heavy breathing. Some guy was breathing into the phone. *(JAN sees the look on Laura's face)* I wasn't imagining it! *(The phone rings again. JAN recoils from the phone. LAURA goes over to it and slowly picks it up. She listens for a moment)*

LAURA. Yes. I'm sorry, she hung up on you. *(To Jan)* It's Greg, he's out of breath. *(Back to phone)* What? You fell in a ditch? Yes ... I'm sure it wasn't there yesterday. Where? The white farmhouse? *(Looks out of the window)* Yes, I can see it. I'll come and pick you up. *(She puts the phone down)* Well, at least you didn't imagine it. *(LAURA gets her coat and starts to leave)*

JAN. Can I come? I hate being left alone.

LAURA. I won't be long.

JAN. Please, Laura. It's just that I feel a bit on edge.

LAURA. I'll only be a few minutes.

JAN. I get these panic attacks. I've always had them. Even when I was a kid my parents could never leave me alone.

LAURA. How do you expect to recover if you always run away from it? Now you stay here and cope...

JAN. How long will you be? God, I wish Greg wouldn't go on these runs.

LAURA. Oh, stop fretting, Jan. *(Sarcastically)* I'll be back before midnight. Just for you. *(There is a knock on the door and GEORGE sticks his head in)*

GEORGE. 'Morning everybody!

LAURA. Ah, it's George. He'll keep you company. *(LAURA exits)*

GEORGE. I brought you some turnips.

JAN. Come in George.

GEORGE. Look, if you ever need anything picked up in the village, you only have to ask.

JAN. That's very kind of you, George, but Laura's just going over to the next farm to pick up Greg. He fell in a ditch apparently.

GEORGE. Just now?

JAN. Yes.

GEORGE. How'd he fall into a ditch in broad daylight?

JAN. He was jogging. You see he sweats a lot and his glasses steam up ... he can't see where he's going. The truth is he needs a lot of looking after. He's been eating these vitamin pills only because he can't cook. All he really cares about are his rocks. *(GEORGE gets hold of the wrong end of the stick. JAN notices this and indicates Greg's rocks)* Rocks.

GEORGE. Ah! Well, I'm sure he cares a lot about you.

JAN. Oh, he probably does. He'd just spend more time with me if I were ten thousand years old. Why don't you sit down, George, and I'll fix you a coffee.

GEORGE. I must admit to a powerful thirst, but the doctor said...

JAN. No coffee.

GEORGE. Quite right.

JAN. Or tea or chocolate.

GEORGE. Very sensitive stomach, you see.

JAN. *(Playing along)* It's a bit early for alcohol, I suppose...

GEORGE. I know, but doctor's orders...

JAN. *(Laughing to herself)* I'll get you some whisky. Would you like some water with it?

GEORGE. I would, but the water 'round here's full of chemicals. It's all the fertilizer we use.

JAN. *(Teasing)* You'd better have it straight then.

GEORGE. You're quite right, I should. *(JAN gets a bottle of whisky and a tumbler)*

JAN. Say when. *(JAN pours a little into the tumbler. GEORGE winks and gestures for her to put a bit more in. She does. GEORGE pulls the same routine again and JAN pours in so much that it overflows)*

GEORGE. When! Whoops! Too much. *(With relish)*

Never mind, I'll force it down. *(JAN puts the whisky away and goes to the stereo)*

JAN. I'll put some music on. *(She puts on a record of soothing classical music, and, almost by habit, grabs her bottle of pills)* Anything interesting on the news this morning?

GEORGE. There was this accident out on the highway near Thornby. One of the McCullogh boys got himself killed.

JAN. Oh, dear.

GEORGE. It's no surprise. They're a damnfool family if you ask me. Robert knew the elder boy, got a lot of idiot notions from him too. Tried to talk him into buying a motorcycle and going to California or somethin' just as stupid.

JAN. Did you talk Robert out of it?

GEORGE. I thumped him out of it. *(An awkward pause)*

JAN. Was there anything else on the news?

GEORGE. Not much. Oh, there was this story from the city you may be interested in. Some kid poisoned his entire family. Bit by bit he poisoned them all by putting antimony in their pills. Turns out antimony can give you what looks like a heart attack but it leaves no trace. He was only caught because the drug store wondered why he kept buying so much of the stuff.

JAN. You mean it's possible to poison someone without a doctor being able to trace it?

GEORGE. That's right. Makes you think, don't it?

JAN. *(Looks at the pills in her hands)* It certainly does. *(JAN gets up and moves nervously around the room)* George. Have you ever been in a situation where you thought something had happened, but ... it hadn't really happened at all.

GEORGE. Seein' things...?

JAN. Like dreams. But you're awake.

GEORGE. Can't say as I have. There's things that exist and things that don't. Ain't nothin' in between.

JAN. *(Almost to herself)* For some people a lot of their life is "in-between". *(To George)* I mean, look at this house! You said yourself people have seen ghosts here.

GEORGE. Oh, that's just talk. I'm sure. You've been watching too much T.V. These ghosts make a good story, but that's all they are. Now you worry about all that *after* you see a ghost — not before.

JAN. You're right ... I'm being silly. Thank you, George.

GEORGE. Well, I should be on my way. Thanks for the ... coffee, eh?

JAN. *(Urgently)* George! *(She is about to say something, but decides against it)* I'm really glad you dropped over. I think of you as my friend.

GEORGE. I'm glad you feel that way.

JAN. Sometimes I get frightened on my own.

GEORGE. I'm just across the road. There's nothin' for you to worry about. Bye for now. *(GEORGE exits. JAN stops the music and then looks closely at the bottle of pills in her hand. She takes one of the pills out and examines it carefully. As she does this the sound of a car can be heard coming up the driveway. She goes to the window and appears to have an idea. She takes some of the pills and stuffs them under the cushion of the sofa, then she lies down and pretends to be passed out. She opens her eyes for a moment and tips over the bottle of pills which she has placed on the coffee table. GREG and LAURA's voices can be heard outside. JAN jumps up and turns the music back on, flops down on the couch, and just before they enter rolls over into the position of someone in a deeply drugged sleep. The door opens and GREG hobbles in being assisted by LAURA)*

GREG. I don't know ... it was a dark patch. I thought it was the road.

LAURA. Just lie down and put your feet up. *(She notices Jan on the sofa)* Jan! Jan, wake up! *(To Greg)* Sit on the chair.

GREG. I'm all right ... really.

LAURA. I'll wake her up. Jan! *(She shakes her)* She's out cold! *(LAURA notices the pill bottle)* Ah! She's been into the pills again.

GREG. *(Worried)* How many did she take?

LAURA. *(Examining the bottle)* Relax. There's only a couple missing.

GREG. Is she breathing? She's still breathing, isn't sh?

LAURA. Take it easy, Greg.

GREG. I don't like this idea of switching the pills. In fact it worries the hell out of me.

LAURA. No-one's going to find out.

GREG. She might notice the diference ... for God's sake, she's flat on her back!

LAURA. Greg... you're getting all wound up. Sit back... relax. *(LAURA runs her hands through his hair and massages his neck)*

GREG. I just wonder ... about all this. She seems so much better.

LAURA. Greg ... she's not "better". They managed to patch her up with four months of therapy, but don't kid yourself it can't happen again. The slightest stress and she'll be gone.

GREG. It's not entirely her fault. If we hadn't met again at the funeral...

LAURA. *(Sharply)* What do you mean by that? You think I caused her breakdown ... is that what you're saying?

GREG. Shhh! *(GREG glances at Jan, but she appears to be still asleep)* No, of course not! But you didn't help either.

LAURA. These depressions are totally self-indulgent. She could fight them, but she won't. If she really cared about you she'd fight them. She knew what you were going through, but she couldn't handle it. Just when you needed her the most she practically went into a coma. All she could do day after day was stare at the wall ... for God's sake, she didn't even know who you were!

GREG. Yes, but she recovered, didn't she?

LAURA. The next time she won't. Greg, she's weak. You've always needed someone strong. Remember, I was the one who cared... I was the one who gave you support and comfort while she was a frothing imbecile! You know in the long run this is the best way. *(She looks intently at Greg. He appears undecided)* Greg! *(He moves away from her)* You don't kiss me anymore.

GREG. *(Whispers intensely)* She's still my wife, you know! *(She looks at him coldly, and moves to the base of the stairs, where she stops and turns)*

LAURA. All right! You want me to go, I'll go! But you'll need my help again someday. Don't forget Mum and Dad are dead, and she's never going to recover. All you have left is me! *(Angrily LAURA runs upstairs. GREG thinks for a moment, and then hobbles after her)*

   GREG. Laura! *(GREG exits upstairs. JAN opens her eyes and slowly looks around. The lights fade. Dramatic music wells up and continues through the blackout until it is replaced by the sound of the wind)*

End of Scene 2

SCENE 3

AT RISE: After the blackout a faint blue light filters in through the windows. It is the middle of the night and a strong wind is blowing outside. Suddenly there is a piercing scream offstage.

   JAN. No! No! Greg! Stop them! Stop them! *(JAN screams again. The voices come from upstairs)*

   GREG. Wake up, Jan!

   JAN. No! No!

   GREG. You're dreaming, Jan. I'll put the light on.

   JAN. Greg?

   GREG. Yes, I'm here. You were dreaming, that's all.

   JAN. Oh, God! It was terrible. *(There is the sound of a door opening upstairs)*

   GREG. Jan ... come back to bed. *(A light goes on on the landing and illuminates the stairs. JAN comes downstairs followed by a sleepy Greg)*

   JAN. I can't rest. When I do manage to fall asleep all I get is nightmares.

GREG. Take one of your pills.

JAN. No. I don't want to go back to sleep. I think I'll stay up for a while. Make some hot chocolate. *(JAN goes into the living room and turns one of the small table lamps on)* Do you want some?

GREG. *(Yawning)* No. *(JAN disappears into the kitchen. LAURA enters from upstairs)*

LAURA. What's all the commotion?

GREG. Dreams.

LAURA. Has she taken her librium?

GREG. No. She doesn't want to, She's going to stay up for a while.

LAURA. It's past five in the morning for God's sake!

GREG. The peace of country living, eh? *(JAN enters and sees Laura)*

JAN. I'm sorry. Did I wake you up as well?

LAURA. No. I just came down to water the plants.

JAN. I'm making some hot chocolate. Would you like some?

LAURA. No thanks. *(LAURA goes back up the stairs and exits)*

JAN. Well, she's mad at me.

GREG. *(Impatiently)* She's not mad at you! She's just not at her best when she's awakened at five in the morning.

JAN. Oh, I see! It's my fault because I woke her up! Well, if she wasn't here I wouldn't be having these damn nightmares! *(JAN exits angrily into the kitchen)*

GREG. Jan...

JAN. *(Talking through the hatch)* How can a guy who is supposed to be so intelligent act so dumb? Can't you see the way she manipulates you? You're blind to everything she does!

GREG. You make me sound like an insensitive clod!

JAN. At last! He understands! *(JAN slams down the sliding hatch. LAURA comes down the stairs with just her satin nightgown on. She has Greg's slippers. He takes them and tries to shoo her back upstairs. She does not leave, but watches Greg with amusement)*

GREG. *(To Jan, through the hatch)* Honey ... do you want to talk?

JAN. *(Offstage)* No!

GREG. Look ... I'm sorry. I'll admit I'm not perfect. In fact I know I'm a bit insensitive sometimes...

LAURA. *(With a laugh)* No kidding. *(GREG gives Laura an exasperated look and indicates for her to go upstairs. She exits upstairs with a smile. GREG turns back to Jan)*

GREG. ... but you've got to give me a chance. *(JAN partially opens the sliding hatch and peers through)*

JAN. What do you want to talk about?

GREG. Tell me about your dream.

JAN. I'd rather not.

GREG. Now, the doctors said...

JAN. Can't you leave the doctors out of this! *(JAN slams the hatch down again)*

GREG. ... that discussing these things helps.

JAN. But you don't understand them.

GREG. I try, don't I? *(After a pause JAN comes out of the kitchen and sits down on the sofa)*

JAN. All right. I was dreaming about spiders. The whole house was surrounded by them. They were getting through cracks and under doors, and they were forcing the bedroom window open. Soon they were crawling all over me and sticking in my windpipe. I couldn't breathe. It was horrible.

GREG. You know, that's interesting.

JAN. Oh, Greg! It was not "interesting".

GREG. It's probably because of that thing in the paper yesterday.

JAN. I didn't read the paper yesterday.

GREG. Oh, it was fascinating. It seems there was this woman...

JAN. Is this going to be gory?

GREG. No. It was amazing, really. This woman had gone on a cruise to the tropics and developed a sore on her face which grew quite large. Then one day it burst and all these spiders popped out. *(JAN stares at him, utterly horrified)* They'd been nesting you see. Nobody knew they could nest like that.

JAN. That's the most horrible thing I've ever heard.

GREG. It's only a story.

JAN. It was revolting!

GREG. *(Shrugs)* I was only trying to help.

JAN. Sure! You're sick! You're the one should see a doctor, not me!

GREG. Jan, we mustn't squabble like this. We came to the country to become close again.

JAN. Then get rid of that damn sister of yours!

GREG. But why?

JAN. Because she hates me.

GREG. Jan, that's nonsense.

JAN. Send her away, Greg. With her here I'll never recover.

GREG. It really means a lot to me that you two patch

things up...

JAN. Greg, do I have to spell it out! I'll never recover with Laura in this house! Get her out of here!

GREG. *(Undecided)* But, what could I tell her?

JAN. The truth.

GREG. I can't do that!

JAN. Then make something up, I don't care! But if she isn't out of here by tomorrow, I'm going to check myself back into the hospital.

GREG. Look, it's the middle of the night, you're upset. It's hardly the right time to go making decisions. *(During this argument a shadow appears on the staircase and moves slowly downstairs. It is the shadow of LAURA)*

JAN. *(Hurt)* You think I can't see what's happening! All I ask is a chance to get things going between us again, but I can't while she's around! How could you possibly bring that woman here knowing how I feel about her? Is it because you don't want to be alone with me ... is that it?

GREG. Of course not. If I didn't want to be with you I would have divorced you.

JAN. You would have divorced me if it hadn't been for my father! *(GREG looks at her, shocked)* It's true, isn't it? He's been very useful to you. Getting you all those research grants and scholarships, to say nothing of all the good connections. Yes, this marriage is very useful to you, but what happens to me when your beloved thesis is finished? I'll be out on the heap with all the rest of those cracked-up and discarded lumps of rock!

GREG. *(Stunned)* You really believe that?

JAN. I'm beginning to.

GREG. Jan, it's just not true. I haven't divorced you because I believe our marriage can work.

JAN. It won't work with her here!

GREG. But, Jan...

JAN. Get rid of her, Greg!

GREG. Please ... be reasonable...

JAN. All right, I'm leaving! You and Laura set up house! *(JAN heads for the door)*

GREG. Will you just listen...

JAN. No, you listen! I'm going back to the hospital and I'm going to check myself in. And you know what that means, don't you? It means I can get out when I feel like it — not when you and Laura feel like it. Where are the car keys? *(GREG looks closely at JAN who rummages through the drawer of Greg's desk looking for his keys. It is obvious she means business)*

GREG. I'll ask her to leave. *(JAN stops searching and looks at Greg)*

JAN. Ask?

GREG. I'll tell her she has to go. First thing in the morning, O.K.

JAN. You won't let her talk you out of it?

GREG. If it helps you recover I'll do it. That's the most important thing.

JAN. Thank you. I'm feeling better already.

GREG. Well, I'm off to bed. Are you coming?

JAN. No, I'm going to stay up for a while.

GREG. Goodnight then. *(GREG moves toward the stairs. He sees LAURA's shadow cast on the wall by the light at the top of the stairs. The shadow moves away. GREG stops for a moment when he sees this, and looks back at Jan who has not noticed it.*

GREG exits upstairs. JAN is about to take her empty cup of hot chocolate into the kitchen when she thinks she hears voices upstairs. She goes to the base of the stairs and the light on the landing goes out and there is silence. JAN thinks for a moment and gets her tape recorder and microphone out and sits down on the sofa)

JAN. Hi, Kate. You won't believe this, but it's five thirty in the morning. I've been having these dreams again. I'm afraid. This will probably make you laugh, but I'm convinced there's a conspiracy against me ... at least I was until now. She's got some strange hold over him which I have no power against, but he's promised me that tomorrow he'll get rid of her. I'm hoping that this will be the end of it. *(Pause)* Kate, they keep telling me that it's my illness coming back, that I'm imagining all this, and the most frightening thing is: what if they're right? *(JAN turns off the tape recorder and puts it away. She gets out a magazine and begins to read it. It is quiet except for the sound of the wind outside. There is a sudden gust and the lights dim momentarily. JAN looks up nervously but relaxes when the lights come back on, and carries on reading. Then there is a distant sound, faint, but rather like a heartbeat. JAN reacts to the sound, but it fades. After a moment the heartbeat sound comes back again, a little louder this time. JAN is getting scared. There is a sudden scratching noise at the window. JAN jumps up and the magazine falls to the floor. She backs away from the window. The scratching starts again, louder this time like fingernails scratching on the glass of the window. JAN is terrified. She moves toward the stairs. She calls upstairs, but not loudly)* Greg! *(There is a sharp noise from the window and JAN turns to see what it is. Suddenly the windows fly open and the curtain billows into the room. As this happens all the lights go out and the only illumination is from the moonlight coming through the win-*

dow. She calls in terror) Greg! Greg! *(A terrifying electronic sound is added to the sound of the heartbeat. In the darkness JAN can be heard tearing through some drawers searching for a flashlight. The heartbeat is quite loud now and faster than before. Finally JAN finds a flashlight and turns it on. She beams it at the window which has slammed closed in the wind. There is no-one at the window. She beams the light around the living room and it too is empty. She moves towards the windows to check, but chickens out and backs away toward the double doors. Suddenly, right in the beam of her flashlight, a figure leaps up from behind the sofa with a long knife in his hand. The figure has an old, dishevelled face and wears a dirty black overcoat. Laughing maniacally, he lunges at Jan with the knife. JAN screams and falls in a faint. The flashlight goes out and all the sounds stop. After a moment Greg's voice can be heard from upstairs)*

GREG. What's the matter, Jan? *(GREG comes downstairs in the darkness and tries to turn the lights on, but nothing happens. In the darkness Laura's voice can be heard)*

LAURA. *(Offstage)* What in Heaven's name is going on now?

GREG. I think a fuse blew, that's all. I'll check the breaker panel. *(GREG, still in darkness, goes to the breaker panel under the stairs. He switches the lights back on. JAN is lying on the floor. Both GREG and LAURA go to her)*

LAURA. Is she all right?

GREG. *(Checks Jan)* Just fainted, I think. *(GREG lifts Jan's head up and tries to revive her)*

LAURA. *(With a faint smile)* I'll get her some water. *(LAURA goes into the kitchen. JAN begins to come around)*

GREG. What happened, Jan? Are you O.K.?

JAN. I saw a man!

GREG. What, outside?

JAN. No! He must have come in through the window. He was old, grotesque ... he had a knife!

GREG. *(Goes to window)* This window?

JAN. Yes.

GREG. But, it's closed. And locked from the inside.

JAN. Then he must be in here somewhere!

GREG. There's no-one here, Jan.

JAN. Check the house! He must have gone into the basement. *(GREG looks at LAURA, hardly concealing his impatience)*

GREG. *(Sarcastically)* To think the old hermit's ghost is probably sitting in our basement.

JAN. *(Angrily)* Greg!

GREG. I'll go and check.

JAN. Well, take the gun for God's sake! I said he had a knife!

GREG. Oh. Yeah.

JAN. You don't believe me, do you? You think I'm having another breakdown.

GREG. *(Gets the shotgun)* I said I'll go and check. Take it easy.

JAN. *(Looks around)* There must be some clues ... footprints ... dirt on the floor. *(JAN goes to the window and pulls back the curtain to check the latch. Just as she does this a face pops into the window and scares everyone)*

MAN. I heard some screams! Anything wrong? *(The man turns out to be George, so everyone relaxes)*

GREG. It's George!

JAN. *(To George)* We had a prowler!

GEORGE. Is that all! Looks more like a py-jama party, don't it! *(GEORGE leaves the window and comes around to the front doors and enters)*

JAN. *(To George)* It wasn't just a prowler. He was in here ... he had a knife!

GEORGE. He got inside! Why that little begger! *(Looks around)* Probably one of the local kids if you ask me. It was that stereophonic system of yours they was after, I'll bet. That's all the kids want these days. Robert was just the same, always pestering me to buy him one. He's in the city now, up to his ass in stereophonic systems no doubt.

JAN. He was hideous to look at ... kind of deformed.

GEORGE. Sounds just like my son! *(He roars with laughter)* Tell you what, I'll go and check outside for footprints. I once read a book by that Sherlock Holmes fella ... the Hound of the Basketballs or something, so I know how it's done, eh? *(GEORGE heads off through the double doors and exits. LAURA gets out her cigarette case)*

LAURA. Will it frighten anyone if I light a cigarette? *(JAN sits sullenly)*

GREG. I hope this puts your fears to rest.

LAURA. No-one is trying to hurt you. If you just took your medication like you're supposed to none of this would have happened.

GREG. Why don't you take your pills now.

LAURA. I'll get them. *(LAURA gets Jan's pills and a glass of water and takes them to her. JAN looks at Laura with great mistrust, and then at Greg for support, but he does not react. JAN reluctantly swallows the pills and drinks the water)*

LAURA. There, you'll feel better in no time. *(There is a knock at the window behind them and George's face appears. He waves at Greg to open the window, which he does. GEORGE sticks his head in)*

GEORGE. The soft earth under a window is the traditional place for footprints to be found. Right? *(He looks)* But in this case there ain't any. However, I got an explanation for that.

JAN. *(Earnestly)* What's that?

GEORGE. *(Deadpan)* I'm standing on concrete. *(He explodes with laughter)* Hey, maybe it was the ghost, eh? Floated right through the wall! *(GEORGE laughs at his joke and then clambers in through the window. He notices how upset Jan is and stops laughing. He tries to reassure her)* Well, there's certainly no-one around now.

JAN. I'm sorry we got you up, George.

GEORGE. That's O.K. I was up anyway. I've got to go down and pick up some seed first thing. If there's any more problems ... well, is that gun loaded?

GREG. Yes.

GEORGE. Use it. Pepper his hide. Give him a little country hospitality. *(Starts to leave)*

GREG. Good night, George.

GEORGE. Goodnight. *(Exits)*

GREG. Well, I think we can all go to bed now. *(To Jan)* Those pills of yours should be working by now.

JAN. I'm not tired.

LAURA. You're not! Well I certainly am. I'll see you in the morning. Good night. *(Exits upstairs)*

JAN. I'm going to stay awake and watch the dawn come up. *(JAN gets the shotgun and sits down with a determined look on her face)*

GREG. *(With a smile)* Jan — you look ridiculous!

JAN. I'll sleep during the day.

GREG. You're going to sit there for the rest of the night cradling a shotgun?

JAN. That's right.

GREG. *(Trying to be patient)* Well, be careful you don't hurt yourself or blow a hole in the wall shooting at some figment of your imagination.

JAN. I want to see if the figment likes lead in its belly.

GREG. *(Shaking his head)* Suit yourself. *(GREG goes upstairs. Once he is out of sight JAN spits out the pills — which she had only pretended to swallow — and hurls them angrily across the room. She moves cautiously around the room with the gun outstretched. She pushes open the swing door to the kitchen and peers in. She looks behind the double doors. She begins to relax a bit, and decides to put on some music. She goes to the stereo and puts on Gordon Lightfoot's "Minstrel of the Dawn". She sits in a chair and listens to the music although she keeps looking around. After a while her anxieties ease slightly, and the music almost lulls her into sleepiness. The sound of the heartbeat returns and JAN immediately tenses up. Then there is a loud noise similar to the one heard earlier, like fingernails on glass. The heartbeats sound even louder and faster. JAN jumps up in terror)*

JAN. Greg! Gre... *(She stops herself as if not even trusting Greg this time. She pulls herself together and her resolve hardens. Purposefully she cocks the shotgun. The noise increases. She aims the gun at the window. Suddenly the lights go out and the music grinds to a halt. This time she does not panic. Once again the windows fly open and the curtains billow inwards. The windows snap closed again. A cloud appears to have obscured the moon as even the moonlight fades, and the room is plunged into almost total darkness. JAN can see nothing. There is a creak on the floorboard)* I can hear you! I can hear you! *(Someone bumps into a piece of furniture)* Don't come any closer! I've got a gun! *(As soon as Jan says this the shotgun goes off with a loud crash and a flash darts across the room from the end of the barrel. There is the sound of the body falling. GREG shouts from the top of the stairs)*

GREG. For God's sake, Jan! *(He blunders downstairs in the dark and tries to turn the lights on)* Just because a fuse blows doesn't mean the house is full of murderers! There must be a short circuit somewhere. *(He goes under the stairs to the breaker panel. After a moment the lights and the music go back on. GREG sees a body lying on the floor, half visible behind the furniture)* Good God! It's Laura! *(GREG kneels and touches the body. He stands up. There is blood on his hands. He turns to Jan)* She's dead. *(Angrily to Jan)* She's dead! *(He moves towards her. She turns and points the shotgun at him. Both freeze. Blackout. Dramatic music punctuates the end of the scene and continues throughout the blackout)*

End of Act I

ACT II
SCENE 1

AT RISE: This scene takes place immediately after the end of the previous scene. JAN is still pointing the shotgun at GREG.

JAN. Keep away from me!

GREG. Jan, she's dead! Can't you see what you've done! *(Looks at the body)* Oh, God, Laura!

JAN. She wanted to kill me and you knew about it!

GREG. She didn't want to kill you! Please, Jan, put that gun down.

JAN. She has a knife!

GREG. What are you talking about! *(Looks)* There's no knife.

JAN. She must have a knife.

GREG. *(Angrily)* She wouldn't try to kill you! *(Looking at the body)* Oh Jesus ... Jesus!

JAN. I've only shot one barrel you know. This gun's still loaded!

GREG. You want to kill me, too? Is that what you want?

JAN. I want to know the truth! What was going on between you and Laura?

GREG. Nothing, damnit! I told you I was going to ask her to leave! Please, Jan, put that gun down.

JAN. Then why did you put poison in my pills?

GREG. *(Taken aback)* Poison?

JAN. Remember when I was out cold on the couch? Well, I was awake and I heard every word you said. *(GREG reacts, but only slightly)* I thought someone had tampered with my pills. I found out I was right.

GREG. It wasn't poison. Laura thought you should have stronger tranquilizers. She said you were beginning to relapse ... that your pills weren't strong enough.

JAN. You were trying to poison me!

GREG. Goddamnit, I wasn't! They were just ... look, I didn't agree with it anyway. You heard that, didn't you?

JAN. Why don't you tell me the truth for once?

GREG. Jan, she's dead! There'll be time for explanations later.

JAN. Later I won't have a gun. *(GREG doesn't know what to say. He moves toward Jan)*

GREG. Jan...

JAN. Get back!

GREG. I don't want to hurt you.

JAN. Then why did you carry on with Laura behind my back? All these years you were lying to me. And while I was in the hospital ... what were you doing then?

GREG. Nothing! We hardly ever saw each other!

JAN. *(Sarcastically)* But who was looking after you? Who cared most for you? Who gave you support and comfort while your wife was a frothing imbecile? And "why don't you kiss me anymore, Greg?" *(GREG bows his head and turns away from Jan. She watches him)* And all those times I asked you what the matter was and you said nothing was the matter, and the doctors said nothing was the matter...

GREG. How could I tell you? You'd have walked right out on me.

JAN. No, I wouldn't.

GREG. If I'd cared less about you it would have been easier. I just couldn't bring myself to tell you, and when she told me she was going out west I thought the whole thing was over. Laura said she wanted to reconcile things with you and I believed her.

JAN. Is that why she came downstairs when the lights went out?

GREG. I heard her walk along the landing. I thought she was going to talk to you. Ask you to let her stay.

JAN. It was completely dark and she crept down very quietly. Now do you see what kind of woman she was?

GREG. Jan, once we got married I told Laura that it was over. I didn't see her again until the funeral.

JAN. I would have understood ... if only you'd talked to me.

GREG. I couldn't. I wanted to talk to you about it, but I couldn't. I was confused. But it really was over. She told me she was going out west. All she wanted was a little time with me to prepare herself emotionally. You've got to believe me, Jan, I still love you. *(JAN lowers the gun and looks sadly at Greg)*

JAN. *(After a pause)* We'd better call the police.

GREG. Yes ... I suppose so. *(They look at each other for a moment)*

JAN. Well, we sure botched up our big reunion, didn't

we? *(JAN finally gives way to tears)* **Oh, Greg, I'm sorry!** *(She pulls herself together)* **Could you phone the police, Greg? I don't think I have the nerve right now.**

GREG. **Jan, I love you. I can't always show it but I do.**

JAN. *(This upsets her even more)* **I'd better go and change.** *(JAN starts to go upstairs)*

GREG. **You realize what this means, of course.** *(JAN stops)* **It's the end of the road for us.** *(JAN turns to Greg)* **They'll put you away for a long time for this.**

JAN. **But surely ... they'll understand...**

GREG. **Understand what? That she was trying to kill you? With what? Where's the knife? Where's the gun? And wasn't it a man you claim you saw? You've been out of the hospital less than a week, what do you expect them to think?** *(A look of anguish crosses Jan's face and she turns and runs upstairs. GREG goes over to the window and looks towards George's farmhouse. He thinks for a long moment)* **Jan! Jan, come down here!** *(JAN appears at the top of the stairs)*

JAN. **What's the matter? Did you phone?**

GREG. **No. Come here!** *(JAN comes downstairs. GREG stares at the body of Laura intensely. JAN sees the expression on his face and backs away from him slightly)*

JAN. **Greg ... what are you thinking...** *(GREG turns and looks at Jan with a steely look in his eyes. JAN reacts to this with apprehension. The lights fade slowly and ominous music is added to the fade and continues through the blackout)*

End of Act II, Scene 1

SCENE 2

AT RISE: It is early evening and the rays of the setting sun are falling across the room. By the end of the scene it will be completely dark outside. GREG is sitting studiously by his "contraption" and has a pair of goggles on. He presses a button and the swinging arm of the device crashes down onto a rock. He pulls the goggles off and examines the rock. He appears angry and throws down his note pad. JAN enters slowly from outside)

JAN. How's it going?

GREG. Annoying. I mean, there are scientific rules... at a given angle of strike the fracture should also have certain fixed properties.

JAN. But they don't?

GREG. No, damnit! Stupid rocks please themselves! They split this way and that. *(GREG pushes the rocks to one side)* It's hopeless ... I just can't concentrate. *(He looks at Jan)* Where have you been?

JAN. Would you like me to make you some coffee?

GREG. No.

JAN. Tea?

GREG. *(Irritated)* I don't feel like anything. I asked where you'd been.

JAN. I've just been outside.

GREG. Have you been in the garden again? I told you to stay away from it!

JAN. I was just ... checking.

GREG. If George sees you fussing around the garden all the time he may suspect something. What's the matter

56

with you?

JAN. I'm sorry. I keep getting the feeling that the body isn't properly covered ... I just can't shake it!

GREG. I buried it plenty deep enough. Now just pull yourself together.

JAN. I had a dream last night that there was a leg sticking out of the earth, and as I covered it with dirt a hand began to stick out. No matter how hard I worked I couldn't keep it covered!

GREG. I'm really getting fed up with your damn dreams!

JAN. How can you carry on like this? There's a dead body out there!

GREG. Oh, for God's sake!

JAN. I've got this terrible urge to see it. I had to stop myself from tearing at the earth with my bare hands.

GREG. That does it, Jan! You're going to have to stay indoors.

JAN. *(Horrified)* No!

GREG. You've got to keep away from that body!

JAN. Please, Greg ... let's leave this house!

GREG. I told you! Once the body's decomposed we can dig up the bones and burn them. We're both accessories to murder now, don't forget.

JAN. I'll go mad if we stay here!

GREG. The point is we've got no choice.

JAN. I've got to do something to calm myself down.

GREG. Take some of your librium. I'm going for a run.

JAN. *(Stops him)* No, Greg ... don't leave me here! It's almost dark!

GREG. Take your damn pills! Those relieve your tension, running relieves mine. *(GREG starts to go upstairs and then stops)* Look, my nerves are pretty raw too. I'm sorry if I seem so irritable, but we'll make it through this. Believe me. *(He holds her)* Just remember what the alternatives are.

JAN. If we could just tell them the truth...

GREG. It's too late now, Jan. *(He looks at her firmly)* You're going to have to get used to that. *(Turns away from her)* I'm going upstairs to change. *(GREG exits upstairs and Jan moves around the room nervously. Suddenly she sees something on the floor and stops dead in her tracks)*

JAN. Greg! Come down here... quickly! *(GREG appears at the top of the stairs)*

GREG. What's up?

JAN. Look at the floor! *(GREG comes downstairs)*

GREG. What is it? Did you spill something?

JAN. No! It's that stain George talked about!

GREG. It's just some damp coming up through the floor.

JAN. I cleaned up every trace of Laura's blood. It's this house, we've got to get out of it!

GREG. It's not blood! How could it be? It doesn't make sense. Laura's body is under the garden. Jan, I buried it myself!

JAN. George said the blood returns whenever there's been a murder. When he sees it he'll know.

GREG. It's not blood! She's been dead a week, for God's sake!

JAN. Then what is it?

GREG. *(Flustered)* Will you just clean it up and stop asking stupid questions. *(GREG exits angrily upstairs to finish changing. JAN gets a cloth and starts to clean it up, but with obvious distaste for the chore)*

JAN. *(To herself)* It sure looks like blood. *(There is a loud knock on the door, and JAN freezes)* Oh, my God! Greg... the door! *(JAN tries to clean up the stain at great speed, but in her panic knocks over things. GREG comes hopping down the stairs half-dressed pulling his jogging pants on)*

GREG. Don't panic! *(GREG trips over his jogging pants — still only halfway on — and falls down the last few stairs. The pandemonium continues until GEORGE finally sticks his head around the door)*

GEORGE. Thought you were having a party in here, judging by all the noise.

GREG. It's nice to see you, George. You haven't been around for a few days.

GEORGE. No, well it's spring, eh? Things are getting busy. By the way, I noticed your vegetable garden on the way in. *(GREG and JAN look at each other in momentary panic)*

JAN. *(Nervously)* What about it?

GEORGE. Comin' up beautifully, much faster than mine. What are you using as fertilizer?

GREG. Just ... natural things, George.

GEORGE. Amazin'. Nothin' special, eh?

GREG. Just manure... some old leaves... anything that will decompose. *(GREG wishes he hadn't said that)*

GEORGE. Well, you've certainly got a green thumb, I'll say that.

JAN. *(Jumps in)* The usual, George?

GEORGE. Wouldn't say no. *(JAN gets GEORGE a shot of*

whisky, while GREG tries to keep George away from the stain)

GREG. Why don't you sit down? *(GREG indicates a chair far away from the stain. GEORGE ignores this and sits on another chair. JAN gives GEORGE the whisky)*

GEORGE. Thanks. You know, it's a shame your sister had to leave so soon. *(JAN and GREG look at each other nervously)* It'll be right pretty 'round here in a couple of weeks. Anyways, I stopped by to tell you I'm going to be away for a couple of days. My brother in Millston is sick so I thought I'd go down and help out.

JAN. That's very nice of you. We'll miss having you around to liven the place up.

GEORGE. Oh, I'm sure you'll get along famously on your own, but I thought I should mention that I let myself in the other day and fixed some of the faulty wiring. You were in the village shopping I think. It's just a patch job, my boy'll fix it up proper when he comes home.

GREG. That's very thoughtful of you, George. Look, I have to dash off to catch the last of the light. Why don't you just relax, have another drink. I won't be too long. *(GREG heads for the door, but JAN grabs his arm. She is obviously terrified of the prospect of handling George alone. They exchange some urgent whispers and then GREG disappears outside. JAN turns back to George, still very nervous)*

GEORGE. This running around. What's it all about?

JAN. Jogging? Just to keep fit, that's all.

GEORGE. He just runs in a big circle, then?

JAN. That's right.

GEORGE. Falls down a lot, don't he? Hardly seems worth it.

JAN. Greg enjoys it. And anyway it keeps his mind off
... other things.

GEORGE. I know what you mean, missus. Physical
work is important for that. If I didn't put in a hard day's
... well, it's been a long time since my dear wife ...
departed.

JAN. Oh, George! I had no idea your wife was dead.

GEORGE. She ain't dead ... just departed.

JAN. That's sad.

GEORGE. Yup. She was a wonderful wife ... the old
bitch.

JAN. Why did she leave?

GEORGE: Didn't like the farm life. Wanted some excite-
ment. The old story.

JAN. *(Looking around)* Well, it is hard living in the country if your heart isn't in it.

GEORGE. Her's sure weren't. I couldn't understand it. I
told her the farm life suited her. Honestly, put her in a
field of cows and it'd take you ten minutes to figure out
which one was her.

JAN. Oh, George! *(She laughs)* She couldn't have been
that bad, surely?

GEORGE. No. She did have some amazing powers.
She'd bring home young shoots, replant them, water
them, talk to them, and the next morning — poof —
they'd be dead! Something she learnt from her mother.
No, if I'd had a wife like you my life would have been very
different.

JAN. Is she in the city now?

GEORGE. Yup. Somewheres.

JAN. Does she see much of Robert?

GEORGE. *(Abruptly)* No. He don't want to see her. *(GEORGE grips the armrest of the chair he is sitting in and feels something)* Hello! What's this? *(He picks an object out of the wood)* It's a pellet. A shotgun pellet. Embedded in this chair.

JAN. *(Nervously)* That's very strange.

GEORGE. It sure is. Here's another one ... and another...

JAN. It's odd you never noticed them before. They may be years old for all we know.

GEORGE. I doubt that. I varnished this chair just before you came. There weren't no pellets in it.

JAN. Oh, really?

GEORGE. Has that gun gone off?

JAN. No. It just stays on the wall. *(GEORGE gets up and looks around)*

GEORGE. There's some more over here. Hmm. They all seem to have come from the same direction. Yup. The gun was probably fired from about... here. Any idea how this could have happened?

JAN. To be honest with you I'm mystified by it all.

GEORGE. Really? Well, as Sherlock Holmes always used to say: "There is but one step from the grotesque to the horrible".

JAN. *(Nervously)* What's that got to do with this?

GEORGE. Nothin! But that's what he always used to say.

JAN. I wouldn't worry about it, George.

GEORGE. I'm sure goin' to look into it for you. It's a strange kettle of fish and no mistake.

JAN. There'll probably be a perfectly good...

GEORGE. I'll just check the gun. *(GEORGE gets the shotgun off the wall and takes the cartridges out and sniffs them. JAN tenses up)* Hmm. Aha. *(Looks down the barrel)* Well. *(Turns to her)* They ain't been fired.

JAN. *(Surprised, but relieved)* I'll ask Greg when he gets back. Perhaps he did it by accident.

GEORGE. Yes. That's probably what happened. *(GEORGE puts the gun back on the wall and starts looking at the pellets again)*

JAN. *(Trying to change the subject)* George, I was wondering if you mailed that package I gave you?

GEORGE. What? Ah, yes, I did. Weighed a ton, what on earth was in it?

JAN. Tapes. Cassette tapes. I recite into them. It's for my therapist. It's a lot easier than writing a letter.

GEORGE. *(Still looking around)* Really?

JAN. It helps me relax. I'm amazed at some of the things I've said on tape — later I often don't even remember saying them.

GEORGE. *(Still preoccupied)* That's very interesting. Look, about this gunshot...

JAN. I wouldn't bother yourself about it, George.

GEORGE. *(Reluctantly)* Well, all right.

JAN. Perhaps you'd like another drink?

GEORGE. No, thank you. I should be on my way, my brother's expecting me.

JAN. Couldn't you stay a little longer? Until Greg gets back?

GEORGE. I can't. I promised I'd be there by suppertime. You'll be all right. *(GEORGE gets his coat)* I'll be back in a couple of days.

JAN. Goodnight, George. *(As soon as GEORGE exits JAN grabs the bottle of whisky and pours herself a large shot. She looks around not quite knowing what to do. Something spooks her and she spins around and stares at the window, but everything is silent. She pours herself another shot of whisky and gulps it down. She moves to the window and looks out to see if she can see Greg, but it is now completely dark outside. She closes the curtains tight and also closes the large double doors. Then she gets her tape recorder and talks into it)* God, how I hate this house when it gets dark. All my senses become hyperactive, my hands tingle, everything seems to buzz. I feel that awful panic spreading through my body. I start to sweat... my head spins, and I know I'm beginning to lose control. With another person in the room it's so different — the small sounds are meaningless. Just a creaking floorboard or a branch tapping on a window. Sounds become ordinary when you have company..I guess that's what loneliness is all about. *(Looks around)* I should do those exercises you showed me. *(Puts the recorder down and does some deep breathing. Suddenly the sound of the heartbeat fades in and then fades away. JAN tenses up. Then there is the sound of the front door opening)* Greg! Is that you? *(She goes to open the double doors but is stopped by a strange sound like a heavy object being dragged along the floor)* Greg? *(There is silence, and then the sound of receding footsteps. JAN rushes to the double doors and locks them. Then a noise comes from the window. JAN looks towards it and then goes to grab the shotgun when she is stopped in her tracks by a strange moaning sound from behind the window. Although the sound is distorted it is like a woman in pain)*

VOICE. Jan! *(The voice trails off in a moan)*
JAN. Who is it?

VOICE. *(Louder this time)* Jan!

JAN. My God. Laura! *(She backs away from the window)* No! *(She tries to pull herself together)*

VOICE. Jan. Open the window! *(There is a scratching sound at the window. JAN grabs her bottle of pills and throws a large number of them in her mouth, spilling some on the floor as she does this. She washes them down with a swig from the whisky bottle. The sound of the moaning continues)* Open the window, Jan ... I must talk to you ... open it. Please!

JAN. Oh, God! Greg, damnit, where are you! *(The noises and scratching get louder as JAN becomes more and more terrified. She screams)* Stop it! Stop it! *(Abruptly the scratching and noises stop. Only the heartbeat remains, but it has a slow hypnotic quality to it. Then the woman's voice can be heard again. This time it can be clearly made out as Laura's voice)*

VOICE. Open the window, Jan ... or I'll be back ... before midnight ... I'll come back ... just for you. Open it! *(JAN is horrified, but mesmerized by the voice and the rhythm of the heartbeat. Slowly JAN is drawn towards the curtains and the heartbeats grow in intensity. JAN gets to the windows and dramatically rips open the curtains. As she does this the heartbeat stops. She looks behind the curtains, but there is nothing there. She closes the curtains. JAN is so relieved she bursts into nervous laughter, and turns away from the window. Just as she does this there is the sound of breaking glass and a hand darts out from behind the curtains and grabs Jan around the neck. JAN screams, breaks free and dashes for the door. She throws open the big double doors and runs right into the half-decomposed body of Laura which is hanging from a rope in the hallway. JAN recoils in horror and faints onto the floor. There is a snap blackout and dramatic music punctuates the end of the scene)*

End of Act II, Scene 2

SCENE 3

AT RISE: During the blackout there is a crash of thunder and the sound of rain. The only light is the faint blue light coming through the window and illuminating the body of JAN as it still lies on the floor. The double doors are closed. After a moment the phone rings and JAN slowly wakes up. She looks around, trying to remember what happened, and is still very groggy from the effect of the whisky and the pills. She picks up the phone.

JAN. Hello? *(Pause)* Hello? *(The caller hangs up. Slowly she puts the phone down. She turns on a lamp and looks at the small clock on Greg's desk)* Quarter to twelve! *(She gets up and moves toward the double doors, then suddenly remembers what she saw behind them and stops. She goes tentatively to the window, opens it and calls out into the darkness)* Greg! Greg! *(There is no answer. She closes the window, locks it, and pulls the drapes closed. She looks around the room nervously and notices that the kitchen hatch is open. Inside, the kitchen is dark. JAN carefully crosses the room and peeks inside the hatch. The kitchen is empty and JAN turns away in relief. At that moment the hatch crashes down by accident. Thoroughly spooked, she dashes to the phone and dials "O".)* Hello, operator? Get me the police! *(As JAN waits on the phone her gaze falls on the double doors and she remembers the body of Laura)* Hello. No officer ... I'm sorry. It was a false alarm. *(JAN puts the phone down and goes to the double doors, but she doesn't have the nerve to open them, so she locks them. Just as she does this there is a crash of thunder and she rushes to her tape recorder, and turns it on)* Kate, I don't know what's going on around here, but I think I'm going crazy...! *(There is*

66

another crash of thunder and the lights dim again. JAN leaves the
tape recorder, and stands, terrified, in the middle of the room. There
is silence. She goes over to the stereo and puts some music on, but
instead of soothing music a strange sound comes out of the stereo.
Long chords of terrifying electronic sound, just like the sound heard
at the first entrance of the hermit. JAN turns the stereo off, but the
sound just continues. She tears out the stereo wires but nothing will
stop the awful sound. Suddenly there is a flash of lightning and a
crash of thunder and all the lights go out and the sound stops. JAN
scrambles around looking for a flashlight and then heads to the
phone book, and then dials, looking around the room nervously)
Hello? Is that the Electric Company? Yes, it's nearly midnight... oh, I'm sorry. You have emergency service, don't
you? It certainly is an emergency! All the electricity's off!
No, it can't wait 'til morning... you want me to spend the
whole night in the dark? Yes. The fifth concession road.,
Yes, the Willowby farm. You know George! Oh, thank
God! The storm must have blown one of the lines down.
(Over-reacts) No! Don't come to the house! *(Tries to cover it)*
I mean ... George just fixed the wiring. Check the lines,
one of the power lines must be down! Don't worry about
the house, George's son Robert is going to check it, so you
needn't ... what's that? *(Listens)* Yes. His son Robert ...
that's what he said. *(Pause, then in horror)* Murdered! Are
you serious? *(Listens, stunned)* How many years ago? Oh,
yes... I must have made a mistake. I'm sorry, I... *(Slowly the*
phone drops from her hand. Suddenly there is a loud crash on the
double doors that shakes the whole house. JAN runs to the doors and
checks that they are locked. Some one is trying very hard to open the
doors. JAN goes for the shotgun which is still mounted on the wall,
but it is just out of her reach. She pulls a chair over to help her reach

it, but there is a crash of flying glass from the window and the head of a shovel can be seen silhouetted behind the curtain. Then a hand reaches in the hole made by the shovel and unlocks the latch on the window, opens it and a MAN clambers into the darkened room. JAN turns her flashlight off and hides. The INTRUDER creeps through the room with the shovel poised to strike. JAN makes a small noise and the INTRUDER leaps at her. She puts on the flashlight and sees it's Greg, covered with mud and with bloodstains on his face) Greg! It's me ... it's me!

GREG. *(Stops just in time)* Jan?

JAN. Yes, it's me!

GREG. Are you all right?

JAN. Where have you been? I've been scared out of my mind!

GREG. I don't know what happened — someone slugged me. Jan, what the hell's been going on here? Why didn't you come looking for me? I could have died out there.

JAN. I took some pills ... they knocked me out.

GREG. I guess you know what's behind that door, don't you? How could you dig her up like that and drag her into the house!

JAN. She's dead?

GREG. Of course she's dead!

JAN. Oh God! Greg ... we've got to get out of here! George must have done this!

GREG. George! What the hell are you...

JAN. You know that son of his he keeps talking about? He disappeared years ago. The locals think he was murdered, but nobody ever found the body!

GREG. How did you find this out?

JAN. I phoned the Electric Company ... I thought the storm had knocked down a power line. George must have set this whole thing up ... the ghost ... the blood! I even gave him all my tapes ... he must know everything!

GREG. It must have been him that slugged me. And he must know about Laura! *(They look around)* Let's get out of here! *(They run to the double doors. GREG stops abruptly)* He may be waiting for us. *(GREG points to the window)* Come on. *(They dash over to the window and throw open the drapes. There is a roar of thunder and illuminated in the flash of lightning is the hideous old man JAN saw in ACT I. He stands on the window ledge and towers over them with a sickle raised to strike. GREG parries with his shovel, but the force of the blow knocks him over the back of the sofa and he falls heavily to the floor. He lies there motionless. JAN rushes to his side and tries to help him. The INTRUDER moves towards her)*

INTRUDER. You would have liked Robert. He was a fine boy. I bought this house for him. He could have taken over the whole farm but he didn't want it. *(The INTRUDER peels his mask off and reveals himself. It is GEORGE)* He wanted to go to the city. Live with that bitch of a mother. Yes, I know you city types, but I don't reckon you're so smart. *(JAN makes a break for the door, but GEORGE grabs her and puts the sickle round her neck)*

JAN. Greg! Greg!

GEORGE. He can't help you. You two are gonna be my masterpiece! With all your psychological problems it'll look just like a murder-suicide. It'll be so perfect I may even give up my job as head ghost. *(GEORGE tightens the sickle around Jan's neck when GREG suddenly leaps out of the shadows and hits George from behind. GEORGE lets go of Jan and*

GREG dashs to the wall and gets down the shotgun. JAN rushes to his side and points the flashlight at George)

GREG. Looks like the tables are turned, George.

GEORGE. You think so, eh? Now if that gun was in your wife's hands I would agree with you, but not yours. I'm a pretty good judge of character as you have seen, and I'd say you're too spineless to fire that thing. Not like your murderous wife. *(GEORGE advances on Greg)*

GREG. Stand back!

GEORGE. Now why don't you just give me that gun?

GREG. Don't come any closer!

GEORGE. Just give it to me, Greg. *(GREG is beginning to panic)* You couldn't tear a hole right through a human being, Greg. That's blood and guts... that's reality, Greg. Can't turn your back on that.

JAN. Don't give it to him, Greg!

GEORGE. *(Almost hypnotic)* It's so easy... *(GEORGE reaches for the shotgun)*

GREG. No! *(GREG fires the shotgun right at George, who spins away with a cry of agony and falls behind the sofa. JAN beams her flashlight at him)* Keep the light on him. I'll check. *(GREG checks George)* He's not breathing.

JAN. We're going to have to call the police now. *(GREG hesitates)* When the police see the mask and the sickle, they'll see what he was up to.

GREG. What about Laura?

JAN. They don't have to know what went on between you. Her death was set up by George and you covered it up to protect me.

GREG. O.K., let's call them. *(GREG picks up the phone when suddenly GEORGE leaps at them from behind the sofa and* *throws GREG to one side. He picks up his sickle from the floor and laughs)*

GEORGE.   Well, the stupid old farmer has outwitted you again. When I checked the shotgun for you earlier, I put in blanks. So easy really. *(GREG grabs the shovel and squares off with GEORGE who menaces him with the sickle. GEORGE swings the sickle at GREG who parries with the shovel. They grapple and separate. Again GEORGE swings and again they grapple. JAN rushes around frantically trying to aim the flashlight to Greg's advantage. With a mighty heave GREG pushes GEORGE backwards and he falls on the sofa. GREG aims a powerful blow at him with the shovel, but GEORGE rolls aside just as the shovel hits the sofa with a mighty thud. GREG chases GEORGE and swings the shovel at him, missing, but demolishing a vase. GREG lunges at George with the shovel, but GEORGE grabs it and swipes at Greg with the sickle. GREG lets go of the shovel and runs away. Gleefully, GEORGE sees that he has the advantage and throws the shovel on the floor and goads GREG into picking it up)*

GEORGE.   There it is, Greg! Go for it! *(GREG tries to pick it up, but GEORGE slashes at him with the sickle and laughs. GREG jumps back)* Go on, Greg! It's right there! *(GREG tries to pick it up again and GEORGE goes for him with the sickle. GREG retreats)*

GREG.   *(To Jan)* Aim it in his eyes! *(JAN aims the flashlight into George's eyes and while he is momentarily blinded GREG grabs the shovel and hits George in the stomach with the handle of the shovel and he sinks to his knees behind the sofa. As he lies there GREG goes wild and brings down the shovel on George with sickening thuds. GEORGE cries out in pain, gives out a final gasp, and then there is silence)*

JAN.   *(Stopping him)* Greg!

GREG.   *(Backs away in horror)* Oh, my God!

JAN. Let's get out of here!

GREG. It's all right, Jan. It's over. *(JAN puts her arms around Greg)*

JAN. Hold me, Greg! This has been such a nightmare! *(GREG caresses her soothingly, but then his hands move slowly up to her neck. JAN reacts)* Greg! What are you doing?

GREG. Nothing darling. Just trying to relax you. *(GREG tightens his grip)*

JAN. You're hurting me!

GREG. Stay calm — you're quite safe.

JAN. Greg! I can't breathe ... Greg!

GREG. You're hallucinating again. Wake up, Jan ... wake up!

JAN. No! *(She breaks away)* Not you, Greg ... no ... not you too! *(She backs away from Greg in horror. GREG picks up the sickle and moves toward Jan with it. When she sees this, something inside her seems to snap and her screams turn into whimpers. GREG aims the flashlight into her eyes which stare wildly, and she becomes strangely quiet)*

GREG. Jan! Jan, look at me! *(There is no reaction. He passes his hand in front of her eyes)* Well, she's gone! Jesus, I thought she was never going to break! Get the lights.

GEORGE. *(From behind the sofa)* You get the lights. *(He gets up)* I'll get the whisky.

GREG. Do as you're told! *(GEORGE sullenly throws the sickle down on the table, takes off his "hermit" coat and throws it on the chair, and opens the double doors. Laura is still hanging there. He tries to ignore her and lumbers offstage to find the breaker panel)*

GEORGE. *(Offstage)* It don't work. Storm must have burnt the damn thing out.

GREG. There's some candles above the fusebox. *(GREG takes the hermit's coat and mask and throws them offstage beyond the double doors. Then he gets a bottle of whisky and a couple of glasses. GEORGE enters with a lighted candle and puts it on the table. They pull up a couple of chairs)*

GREG. Have a drink, George. *(GREG pours a drink for George and one for himself. GEORGE gulps down the whole glass)*

GEORGE. Thanks. Good stuff this. Well, everything went according to plan.

GREG. Yes. Although I didn't think we'd have to go this far. I thought she'd freak out when she saw the body, especially hearing Laura's voice. My God, we spent hours working on those tapes! She just wouldn't break ... not until she knew I was part of it. That was a big risk, George. I don't know what we'd have done if she'd hung on much longer.

GEORGE. *(Pours himself another drink)* I still don't know why you wanted to do it. She seemed so harmless.

GREG. Of course you don't understand! You're a failure! Your wife deserted you, your son deserted you, or tried to anyway. How could you possibly understand someone like me! These bitches never left me alone. Laura picked up where my mother left off, and Jan — well, I admit I married her for less than romantic reasons. I always thought they'd end up destroying each other given half a chance. But it wasn't until I discovered Robert's body in the quarry that I realized I had everything I needed. The perfect house and a rather less than perfect accomplice.

GEORGE. You're a real bastard.

GREG. I'm not a murderer. Not like you, George.

GEORGE. The hell you're not! I got mad... I went crazy. I don't even remember doing it. But you ... you've been planning this for months. You killed your own sister in cold blood!

GREG. I didn't kill her. I didn't pull the trigger.

GEORGE. Laura thought there were blanks in that gun. You told her all she had to do was a little scare job. If I'd known she was going to get killed I'd have had no part of it.

GREG. (*Mockingly*) Poor Laura. I really should have checked the gun more carefully. You see, George, smart people never do anything that they can get other people to do for them. Just think of all this as an experiment in scientific probabilities.

GEORGE. Well, I hope you're happy. Just give me my money and let me get out of here!

GREG. Bit of a problem there, George. (*GREG starts laughing to himself*)

GEORGE. What do you mean ... we agreed ... twenty thousand.

GREG. (*Explodes with laughter*) I don't have that kind of money! God, you're stupid! Why do you think we've been doing this whole charade? So I can keep playing the poor long-suffering son-in-law without her around my neck! (*His laugh becomes quite demented*) I don't have a cent, George! Without my scholarships I'd have to go out and "work" for a living! (*GREG laughs cynically*)

GEORGE. You were lying to me all along!

GREG. (*Imitating George*) Yup! Yuup! I was! It was wrong of me I know, but I thought "why pay all that money to a guy who goes around murdering kids!" (*GEORGE grabs the suckle which is lying on the table)*

GEORGE. I'll kill you for that! *(GEORGE lunges at Greg but suddenly goes weak at the knees, and a look of horror crosses his face. GREG cackles with laughter when he sees this. GEORGE slumps to the ground. GREG holds up his glass of whisky)*

GREG. Great stuff this, eh, George? Antimony. Leaves no trace, remember? You see, after you tried to scare my poor wife and I as the old hermit, the strain was just too much. Your heart just couldn't take it. And remember Laura? As I recall she left a week ago to go out west, and wasn't it you who gave her a ride to the bus stop? Yes, I believe it was! And when they find her body buried next to Robert's in the quarry, well, I don't need to tell you what they'll think. You've been a naughty boy, George, but you're about to become part of the perfect crime. *(GEORGE gives out a final gasp and dies)* Posthumously, of course. *(GREG looks around contently)* Well, I guess there's just one more job for the old hermit to do. *(GREG takes the candle and heads through the double doors. He stops and looks at Laura's dangling body)* Hang in there, Laura! *(He laughs)* I'm going to take you to meet Robert. You'll like Robert, he's just your type.*(He exits chuckling to himself, and puts the hermit costume on in the darkened hallway. He laughs triumphantly and makes ghostlike noises)* Wooo ... open the window, Jan! *(He finds this very amusing)* I'll be back before midnight ... just for you! *(He laughs hysterically at this, comes back into the room dressed in the hermit's mask and coat, continues to make ghostlike noises, and laugh. Suddenly JAN leaps out of the shadows with a Stone Age axe which she has taken off the wall and drives it into Greg's back. GREG takes the mask off)* Jan...! *(GREG turns to reveal the axe embedded deeply in his back. He looks at Jan and staggeringly advances on her, his hand grasping for her throat.*

JAN looks at him in horror and backs away, but just as he reaches her, he collapses, dead, on the sofa. JAN looks at him, not quite knowing what to do. She moves toward the phone when she sees a small red light in the darkness. It is the small portable tape recorder that she had put on earlier in the scene. It is still recording. She picks it up, rewinds it, and presses the "play" button. The following conversation can be heard)

GREG. *(On tape)* ...these bitches never left me alone! Laura picked up where my mother left off, and Jan, well, I admit I married her for less than romantic reasons. I always thought they'd end up destroying each other given half a chance. But it wasn't until I discovered Robert's body in the quarry... *(JAN turns the tape recorder off and goes to the phone and dials)*

JAN. Get me the police! *(The lights fade, JAN blows out the candle)*

THE END

SPECIAL NOTE

A seventeen page technical manual prepared by the author is available. This detailed "how to" includes numerous diagrams and hints on production. It can be obtained by sending $3.00 plus postage to Baker's Plays, 100 Chauncy St., Boston, MA 02111.

MUSIC USE NOTE

Licensees are solely responsible for obtaining formal written permission from copyright owners to use copyrighted music in the performance of this play and are strongly cautioned to do so. If no such permission is obtained by the licensee, then the licensee must use only original music that the licensee owns and controls. Licensees are solely responsible and liable for all music clearances and shall indemnify the copyright owners of the play(s) and their licensing agent, Samuel French, against any costs, expenses, losses and liabilities arising from the use of music by licensees. Please contact the appropriate music licensing authority in your territory for the rights to any incidental music.

IMPORTANT BILLING AND CREDIT REQUIREMENTS

If you have obtained performance rights to this title, please refer to your licensing agreement for important billing and credit requirements.